WELCOME TO
PASSPORT TO READING
A beginning reader's ticket to a brand-new world!

Every book in this program is designed to build read-along and read-alone skills, level by level, through engaging and enriching stories. As the reader turns each page, he or she will become more confident with new vocabulary, sight words, and comprehension.

These PASSPORT TO READING levels will help you choose the perfect book for every reader.

READING TOGETHER
Read short words in simple sentence structures together to begin a reader's journey.

READING OUT LOUD
Encourage developing readers to sound out words in more complex stories with simple vocabulary.

READING INDEPENDENTLY
Newly independent readers gain confidence reading more complex sentences with higher word counts.

READY TO READ MORE
Readers prepare for chapter books with fewer illustrations and longer paragraphs.

This book features sight words from the educator-supported Dolch Sight Words List. This encourages the reader to recognize commonly used vocabulary words, increasing reading speed and fluency.

For more information, please visit passporttoreadingbooks.com.

Enjoy the journey!

Little, Brown and Company
Hachette Book Group
1290 Avenue of the Americas, New York, NY 10104
Visit us at LBYR.com

First Edition: September 2017
Little, Brown and Company is a division of Hachette Book Group, Inc.
The Little, Brown name and logo are trademarks of Hachette Book Group, Inc.

The publisher is not responsible for websites (or their content) that are not
owned by the publisher.

Library of Congress Control Number 2017939182

ISBNs: 978-0-316-26088-6 (pbk.), 978-0-316-47211-1 (ebook),
978-0-316-47212-8 (ebook), 978-0-316-47210-4 (ebook)

Printed in the United States of America.

CW

10 9 8 7 6 5 4 3 2

Passport to Reading titles are leveled by independent reviewers applying the standards
developed by Irene Fountas and Gay Su Pinnell in *Matching Books to Readers: Using
Leveled Books in Guided Reading*, Heinemann, 1999.

DINOTRUX

THE SNOW BLAZERS

Adapted by
Justus Lee

LITTLE, BROWN AND COMPANY
New York   Boston

DreamWorks

DINOTRUX

Attention, DINOTRUX fans!
Look for these words
when you read this book.
Can you spot them all?

snow

cave

rock

skid

The Dinotrux are
lost in the snow.
They need to get home.

Ty asks Revvit for directions.
"That way," Revvit says.

Ton-Ton loves the snow.
Skya does not.

Skya is too tall,
and she cannot see.
Skya lowers her head.
"I am going to get cramps,"
she says.

Ty hears a rumbling.
A big pile of snow is
rushing toward the Trux!
How will they escape?

CLANG!

Someone pushes the group out of the way. They are safe now.

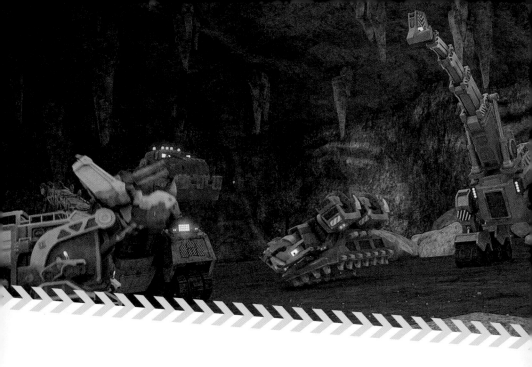

The Trux are inside a cave.

Who saved them?

A Dinotrux comes out.

"My name is Snowblazer."

She turns to a rock on a ledge.

"And this little spitfire is Herb!"

"The Plowasaur is a distant relative
of the Dozeratops," Revvit says.

"Really distant," Dozer adds.
"We have to head south
to get home," says Ty.

Snowblazer offers to help Ty
and his friends.
Ty is very thankful.

Snowblazer leads the Dinotrux through the snow.

The group reaches
Avalanche Canyon.
They need to go down,
but it is a very long way!

"This is the best path," says Snowblazer.

Revvit has a plan.

They will make snow skids!

"Let's trux it up!"

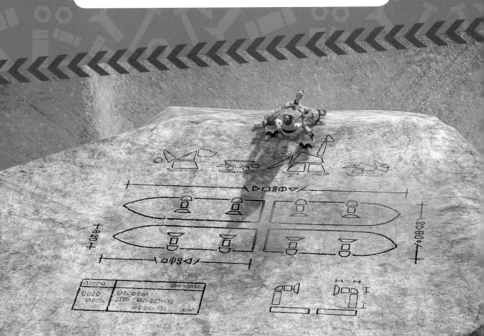

Everyone is ready.

Well, everyone except Skya.

She is afraid.

"Ton-Ton, I cannot do this."

Ton-Ton believes she can.

"Doing something new can be scary,"
he says, "but making mistakes is fun!"

Skya joins the group.
The Trux slide down
the path in a zigzag.

24

One of Skya's skids breaks off.

Ton-Ton comes to help her.

Hooray!

There is no stopping them now!

"Dude, it is all good!
Slow and steady," Ton-Ton says.
Skya rides on her good tread.

Skya skids easily down the path.

She is doing a great job!

Ty hears a rumbling and
looks behind him.
A giant avalanche is on its way!

The Trux skid as fast as they can.

Oh no!

Snowblazer has lost Herb!

But Skya saves Herb before
he is buried in all the snow.

Skya is a hero!

She faced her fear
and saved the day!